FIRST HARVEST

THE LAST THANKSGIVING
BOOK 1

MIRA HALDEN

WINTER, 1913 – NEW YORK CITY

They arrived with frost on their eyelashes and the smell of salt still clinging to their coats.

Yusuf gripped Anya's hand as if she might drift away, swept off by the tide of people pouring onto Ellis Island's cold stone floors. Her fingers were red and swollen from the Atlantic crossing, knuckles raw from clinging to railings and prayer. The ship had been a creaking coffin, rocking through the gray sea for fourteen endless days, and now that it was over, America loomed like a riddle: cold, sharp, vast.

Anya coughed into her handkerchief, folding the sound into the crook of her elbow, but not quickly enough. A man in uniform turned his head.

Yusuf tensed.

"No trouble," he whispered in their shared tongue, barely audible above the din of babies crying and boots scraping across wet stone. "We're here now. We begin."

She nodded, though tears burned behind her eyes. She had held them back since they passed the coastline, when the gray hulk of Lady Liberty rose from the mist like a promise no one could touch. But now, in the harsh fluorescent light of the processing hall, it all crashed in—what they'd left behind, what they'd risked, what they might never see again. Home was not a place they could return to. Only forward now.

They were given numbers. Herded into lines. Eyes checked. Tongues examined. Teeth inspected like livestock. Yusuf's broad shoulders and farmer's hands marked him as "fit for labor." He answered every question in slow, accented English, just as they had practiced. The man in the gray vest nodded once. A stamp hit the paper.

Anya was not so lucky.

They pulled her aside for "further observation," her cough raising suspicion. Yusuf shouted something—a protest, a plea—but was silenced by a thick arm across his chest. She was led away, head down, the blue of her shawl flickering in the crowd like a vanishing bird.

They were apart for twenty hours. To Yusuf, it was longer than the voyage itself. He waited outside the medical wing until his knees ached from standing, until the lanterns dimmed, until he could see nothing but the cold stars blinking above the island's roof.

She was released just after dawn. Her eyes were hollow, but she smiled for him, and that was enough. They walked out together, clutching the few things they had: a canvas satchel with three dresses, Yusuf's folded work papers, a cloth-wrapped bundle of dried herbs and seeds from Anya's mother's garden, a worn folktale book with gold edges, and a silver locket she never opened in front of him.

In America, they were nobody. In their old life, Yusuf had been a schoolteacher's son, and Anya had sung in her church's choir. Now, they were shadows.

They took the train to a neighborhood where the streets stank of coal and wet laundry. The tenement was narrow, loud, and alive with strange smells—cabbage and kerosene, fish and frying dough. Their room was three flights up and just wide enough for a cot and a window.

That night, Yusuf lay beside her on a straw mattress, staring at the cracked ceiling. Outside, a man sang in a language neither of them recognized. Somewhere nearby, a baby wailed, sharp and sudden.

Anya turned to him.

"We'll need coats," she said. "Real ones."

"I'll find work tomorrow."

They didn't speak again for a long while. Her body was trembling against his—whether from cold or fear, he didn't ask.

By week's end, Yusuf was hauling meat carcasses through the back of a slaughterhouse on the edge of the city. His hands grew stiff and purple from the cold, the blood crusting beneath his fingernails no matter how long he scrubbed. The foreman called him "Joe." He didn't correct him.

Anya scrubbed floors and washed linens in a boardinghouse run by a widow with sharp eyes and a heavy cane. On her lunch breaks, Anya hid behind the kitchen's back door and unwrapped her cloth bundle. Inside: dill seeds, rosemary, and dried chamomile—gifts from her mother's hands, folded in a prayer and sealed with hope.

She found a rusted tin pail behind the building and filled it with soil from a nearby alley. One by one, she pressed the seeds into the dirt with her thumb, whispering to them in her mother tongue. She set the pail on their windowsill, the only spot in their room where the light lasted past noon.

It snowed the next day.

Not the powdery snowfall of her childhood, but thick, brutal ice that numbed her cheeks and stole the breath from her lungs. Yusuf came home soaked and shivering, his coat torn at the elbow. He was bleeding from a nick across his palm, but he didn't mention it. Anya boiled water and bathed the wound in silence.

Their supper that night was broth made from bones she had begged from the kitchen. They dipped stale bread into it and shared the silence like a hymn. The tin pail sat untouched on the windowsill, waiting.

As the wind howled through the cracks in the window frame, Anya reached across the table and touched Yusuf's hand.

"Next year," she said softly, "we'll have a real table."

He looked at her, eyes rimmed with red, jaw clenched from the day's weight.

"And a feast," he added.

They said nothing more. But somewhere in the quiet, Anya's seeds waited beneath the soil—patient, hidden, alive.

WINTER, 1914 – TENEMENT LIFE

The windows sweated in the cold. On the inside, droplets ran like melted candle wax down the cracked glass, painting ghostly lines over the view beyond—coal smoke curling from rooftops, laundry frozen stiff on lines, children kicking tin cans in the street below with red, ungloved hands.

Inside their room, the air smelled faintly of boiled onion and soap. The walls were so thin Anya could hear the woman next door scolding her husband in Greek, pots banging like punctuation marks. Somewhere above them, a baby was teething, its shrill cry a steady reminder that life was happening all around them—noisy, needy, relentless.

Yusuf was late that night.

Anya sat at the small table beside the window, rubbing her thumb over a bruise on a turnip. She had bartered two hand-sewn kerchiefs and a basket of laundered linens for it—lumpy, soft in spots, but still enough to flavor a stew. The bread from the bakery down the alley had gone stale overnight, but she had plans for that too.

She lit the stove and filled a dented tin pot with water, watching as the flame flinched beneath it. Then, with a reverence that bordered on sacred, she took down the jar of crushed garlic from the shelf, the one she refilled grain by grain from kitchen scraps. The turnip she peeled with the edge of a broken knife. The bread she soaked in warm broth and gently wrung dry like an old rag, careful not to tear it.

The tenement was a living creature: always shifting, always speaking.

People didn't knock. Doors stayed ajar. Everything was shared— curses, recipes, rumors. On the floor below lived a boy who had lost two fingers to a printing press and now delivered newspapers with a thick accent and a crooked smile. A violinist from Minsk played for coins near the stairwell on Sundays, and his music wept through the floorboards like rain.

And there was Rosa, with her hands always full and belly always round. She had been one of the first to speak to Anya, to press a bruised apple into her palm without ceremony.

"Don't ask. Just eat," she'd said.

It had made Anya want to cry, not for the fruit, but for the way it reminded her of her sister—soft-hearted, no-nonsense, gone.

Now, Rosa knocked with her foot and burst in, her youngest balanced on one hip, a bowl of something steaming in her other hand.

"Try this," she said, setting it on the table without waiting for permission. "Don't smell it first. It's better that way."

Anya obeyed. It was sour and heavy and strangely comforting. She didn't ask what was in it.

"Your man still at the slaughterhouse?" Rosa asked, bouncing the baby on her hip.

"Yes."

"Mine drives a trolley full of ghosts. Swears it talks to him through the brakes." She laughed, then sighed. "You're too quiet. That's not good here. The quiet ones get stepped on."

"I don't need much noise to remember who I am," Anya said.

Rosa studied her for a moment, then nodded approvingly. "You're steel wrapped in silk. That's good. That's useful."

When she left, Anya sat a little straighter.

That night, Yusuf returned later than usual, shoulders slumped, boots soaked through. He limped slightly and winced as he sat.

"They moved me to the saw room," he said. "It's colder, and they shout more."

He didn't say what had happened. He didn't have to. She poured him a cup of weak broth and slid a piece of bread across the table. It was warm and spongy from being re-steamed, topped with sautéed garlic and the tiniest sprinkle of salt she had stolen from the boardinghouse kitchen.

He took a bite and closed his eyes.

"This is bread?" he asked softly.

"It used to be," she said, smiling faintly.

They ate in silence, then shared a cup of tea brewed from crushed lemon peels and dried mint leaves salvaged from the market gutter. It was bitter, but warm. Real warmth, not the kind you imagine.

Later, she pulled the tin pail closer to the window, checking the soil again with bare fingers. Still no sprouts, but the dirt was damp and rich now. She sang to it softly—half lullaby, half prayer. A song her mother had sung when planting onions, simple and rhythmic, full of whispered hopes.

When Yusuf saw her hunched beside the window, covered in candlelight, he said, "You look like a saint."

"I look like a farmer's daughter," she said. "Because I am."

Sunday came, and with it, stillness.

The factory was closed. The boardinghouse work lightened. Anya used the time to wash their few clothes by hand, hanging them near the stove to dry. She took out the silver locket from the wooden box beneath the bed. Inside was a tiny, smudged photo of a boy in a scarf —her younger brother. Left behind.

Yusuf watched her, sitting on the edge of the bed with his hands wrapped in gauze.

"We'll send for him," he said.

"You don't have to promise things we can't afford."

"I'm not promising. I'm planning."

She closed the locket and slid it back into the box.

"Then plan quickly," she said. "He doesn't know how to wait."

That evening, Rosa returned with her oldest child—Eli, barely ten, but already speaking faster than the grown men on the street. He brought Anya a storybook he had outgrown, pages dog-eared and stained. She accepted it with reverence.

"You can read?" he asked her, skeptical.

Anya opened to the first page and began to translate softly, one sentence at a time, from English to her native tongue, then back again. Eli's mouth fell open.

"She's magic," he told his mother.

"No, child," Rosa said, pulling him close. "She's just remembering out loud."

The next morning, a sprig of green broke through the soil in the tin pail—delicate, defiant.

Anya kissed her fingers and touched the leaf.

It was dill.

A single thread of home, finding its way in a place that had forgotten what softness looked like.

LATE AUTUMN, 1914 – TENEMENT LIFE, NEW YORK

The notice came home in Eli's pocket, folded neatly in half and stained with ink.

"Thursday, November 26: Thanksgiving Holiday – No School."

Anya read it aloud at the kitchen table, turning the word over in her mouth like a foreign coin.

"Thanksgiving?" she asked, careful with the syllables.

Rosa snorted from the doorway, her arms full of firewood.

"It's the day Americans eat too much and pretend they're thankful for things they complain about the rest of the year."

Anya tilted her head. "Is it religious?"

"No. Worse—**patriotic**." Rosa dumped the firewood into a crate beside the stove. "They say it's about pilgrims and Indians and surviving a hard winter, but really it's about turkey and pie. You'll see. The markets will be madness."

That week, Anya watched the neighborhood shift.

The shop windows bloomed with painted leaves and signs advertising pumpkin and cranberry and giblet gravy—words she didn't yet know, flavors she couldn't imagine. Even the butchers tied bows around their pigs and geese. In the tenement halls, women argued over whose cousin was coming from New Jersey, who had a real table, who had to borrow chairs from the parish basement.

At the factory, Yusuf came home with news of his own.

"They gave us Thursday off," he said, sitting down to remove his boots. "But they're making us work twelve hours on Friday. Half pay."

Anya stirred the pot of cabbage on the stove and said nothing.

"They call it Thanksgiving," he added. "But for who?"

That night, as Yusuf slept, Anya unwrapped a package she had hidden under their mattress.

Inside were her savings: a few crumpled dollars and a handful of coins, wrapped in an embroidered cloth she had brought from her mother's linen chest. She counted carefully, then tied the bundle again, tight.

The next morning, she walked to the market before the frost had melted, navigating between wooden carts and crates of potatoes piled high. The air smelled of cinnamon and coal smoke. She bought half a chicken, one sweet potato, and a cracked jar of pickled beets. From a stall at the edge of the alley, she found a bruised apple and three sprigs of something green that reminded her, faintly, of home.

She had never seen a turkey up close. The man at the butcher's waved a raw one at her with a laugh.

"Too big for you, little bird," he said, teeth yellow and gapped.

She smiled politely and left with her bundle tucked tight beneath her coat.

Back in the apartment, she cleaned the chicken with salt and hot water, humming under her breath as she peeled and sliced. The sweet potato she roasted with sugar scraped from the bottom of a jar. The beets she folded into warm bread dough, letting the juice bleed into swirls. It wasn't a feast, but it was something made with intention —sacrifice, even.

From her pail, she cut the freshest sprigs of dill and rosemary.

As the apartment filled with the scent of roasting, Anya lit a small candle and cleared the table of Yusuf's papers and the sewing she had promised Rosa. She laid down the best cloth they owned: pale ivory, stained faintly in one corner, but smooth. She placed two mismatched plates and their only good knife.

Then she waited.

Yusuf entered an hour later, smelling of metal and sweat.

"What is this?" he asked, eyebrows raised. "You cooked?"

She gestured toward the table. "It's... Thanksgivink."

He laughed. "That's not a word."

"It is now."

He approached warily, removing his coat. "What's in the bread?"

"Beet. Sweet potato. Dill."

He sat down, scanning the table. "You didn't have to do all this."

"I wanted to."

He looked at her then, as if trying to read something she hadn't said.

"Why?" he asked.

Anya folded her hands in her lap.

"Because if I don't take root here, I will blow away."

They ate slowly, cautiously.

Yusuf chewed in silence for a while, then nodded. "The bread is strange. But good."

Anya smiled. "Like me."

He reached for her hand across the table.

"No," he said. "You are better than strange. You are... stubborn."

She laughed quietly.

Outside, the hallway echoed with music—someone playing harmonica, a pot clanging down a stairwell, children yelling in broken English and older tongues. Rosa shouted something from down the hall that made her children roar with laughter.

Yusuf shook his head. "This isn't our holiday."

"Not yet," Anya said.

They sat in the warmth of their borrowed feast, candlelight flickering between them, a single dill plant swaying gently on the windowsill.

And in the stillness, Thanksgiving became something else entirely:

Not a story about pilgrims or flags, but about presence. About claiming space.

About saying: *We are still here. We are still hungry. But we are together.*

LATE WINTER, 1915 – TENEMENT LIFE, NEW YORK

The pain started like a dull ache in her lower back.

Anya didn't speak of it at first. She swept the floor and boiled onions as usual, breathing through the pulses that came and went like the tide. Her fingers trembled when she lifted the kettle. She told herself it was nothing. Just tiredness. A shift in the weather.

But by evening, her legs could barely carry her.

She lowered herself to the bed slowly, the room spinning, Yusuf's voice distant in the hallway. When he entered—arms full of kindling and face lined with soot—he stopped cold at the sight of her pale face and the wet spot blooming beneath her on the sheets.

"Anya—"

"I think I'm losing it," she said flatly, eyes fixed on the ceiling. "Our baby."

Blood pooled on the floorboards, dark and surreal.

Yusuf carried her to the washbasin, his hands slipping on her arms, his own panic threatening to drown them both. He shouted down the stairwell for help. Rosa came running with towels. Someone sent for the building's doctor—a man who smelled like liniment and liquor and wore his spectacles low on his nose.

He examined Anya with the indifference of someone who had seen too many immigrant women bleed into old blankets. "She'll recover," he muttered, packing his tools. "But she should stay off her feet. And she'll need heat."

He left as quickly as he came, boots clicking down the hallway.

Rosa stayed long enough to light the stove and press a cloth to Anya's forehead.

"She's strong," Rosa said to Yusuf. "But don't leave her alone. Not for a while."

Yusuf nodded, swallowing grief like hot coal.

The room grew quiet again.

Anya lay still, pale and sweat-slicked, one hand resting lightly on her belly. It no longer felt like a secret waiting to bloom. It felt like a betrayal.

She had imagined a child with her eyes and Yusuf's stubbornness. A cradle made from scrap wood, a lullaby sung softly in her mother's language. She had already whispered to it at night, when Yusuf slept —promises she hadn't realized were real until they broke.

Now, there was only absence. A kind of silence that echoed inside her ribs.

For days, Yusuf moved around the room like a shadow.

He cooked what little food they had, changed the linens without comment, and sat beside her in the evenings, fingers twitching uselessly in his lap.

He tried to pray, but the words didn't come. Not in any language.

Instead, he remembered: his father's face at the border, the sound of gunfire echoing through trees, the final time he saw his younger brother—hair matted with rain, eyes full of unspoken goodbye. Yusuf had known loss. But never like this.

This was smaller. Quieter. And somehow, worse.

Anya woke crying on the third night.

The sound startled them both. Yusuf took her into his arms, and she clung to him, face pressed against his collarbone, her shoulders shaking in silent sobs.

"I should have known," she whispered. "My body... it knew. It failed."

"No," he said, too quickly. "Don't say that."

"I couldn't keep it safe. Not even inside me."

He kissed the top of her head and held her tighter, as if he could press her back together.

"It's not your fault," he said again. "It's this place. The cold. The hunger. The fear."

She said nothing.

But in the stillness, Yusuf realized something. It wasn't just the child they had lost. It was a version of themselves they'd been building—one that believed this new life might be generous. That belief had bled out with the baby.

As spring approached, slowly and half-heartedly, Anya began to rise again.

Her movements were slow. Her eyes carried a shadow. But she returned to her sewing, to the boardinghouse on Tuesdays, to the stove. She never mentioned the baby again, not aloud. But Yusuf caught her once holding a blanket she had knitted in secret, pressing it to her face as if to memorize its softness before it disappeared.

In the weeks that followed, Yusuf brought home a gift.

A single packet of real tea—**chamomile**, with faded print on the label and a smell that reminded Anya of her grandmother's kitchen.

He placed it on the table like an offering. She stared at it for a long moment, then set the kettle to boil.

They drank it in silence, both of them cradling their mugs with two hands, letting the steam touch their faces.

"It tastes like... peace," she said.

"No," Yusuf replied. "It tastes like how peace might begin."

On the last Thursday of March, Anya lit a candle at dinner.

She served bread and cabbage stew. Yusuf didn't ask why there was a tablecloth, or why she had added a pinch of sugar to the tea.

"This is our little Thanksgiving," she said softly. "Not for the baby. Not yet. But for surviving."

He nodded. "For still being here."

"For the next seed."

The tradition began that night—not with turkey or stuffing or pilgrims, but with a single flame, a bitter cup of tea, and two people who had learned how to lose together.

Later, when Leah would ask how Thanksgiving became "the family thing," no one would remember this moment exactly. But it began here. In loss. In ritual. In love that refused to die.

SPRING–SUMMER, 1915 | NEW YORK CITY

The baby didn't come. But something else did.

After the miscarriage, Yusuf returned to work with a silence that unnerved the men around him. He spoke only when spoken to. His body moved like a clock wound too tightly. At home, he folded his shirts with military precision, as if control over cloth could compensate for the things he could not fix.

One morning in late April, the factory foreman handed him a folded envelope—creased, smudged, bearing no return address. Just a name written in small, precise script: "**Yusuf Halem.**"

Yusuf turned it over slowly, heart ticking.

The letter was from *Kerem*—his cousin, or something close to it. They had grown up side by side, though the exact relation had long been blurred by war, bloodshed, and the slow unraveling of record books back home. Kerem had been left behind when Yusuf boarded the ship to America. Too young, too sick, or perhaps too afraid. Yusuf had never known the real reason.

The letter was written in their native tongue, in tight script that looked rushed. Kerem was alive. And desperate.

He was in Marseille, working odd jobs and hiding from military conscription. Europe was on fire, and it was spreading. There were rumors he'd been involved in an underground printing press—anti-government leaflets, union propaganda. He didn't say it outright, but Yusuf could read between the lines.

"If you can find a way, I will come. Even as someone else."

Beneath the signature was a single sentence:

"Tell them I am your brother. Your mother had two sons. No one in America knows the truth."

Yusuf folded the letter and put it beneath his mattress.

For three nights, he said nothing.

On the fourth, as Anya slept beside him, her breath even and low, Yusuf sat up and stared at the wall. The coal stove glowed faintly. The locket sat on the table beside her, open just enough for the photo inside to show. He picked it up and closed it gently.

He thought of Kerem, of their last meal together—hard-boiled eggs and flatbread, eaten in silence as they watched soldiers pass through the village square. He remembered the day they had buried his uncle with no coffin, just a blanket and three whispered prayers. He remembered promising he would send for Kerem "soon."

He also remembered what the inspector had said at Ellis Island: *"Clean identity. No lies. No papers, no passage."*

But here in America, clean wasn't always possible. Or affordable.

In the weeks that followed, Yusuf began asking quiet questions.

He found a man in the neighborhood known only as *Nico*—a small, wiry man with ink-stained fingers and a knack for forged letters. Nico spoke seven languages and had papers for all of them. His tiny office above a fishmonger reeked of brine and burned wax.

"Brother, cousin, nephew—I can make anyone family," Nico said with a grin. "Just need the fee. And a story you can remember."

Yusuf hesitated. "It's not a lie. Not entirely."

Nico shrugged. "They never are."

The cost was more than Yusuf could afford. He worked Sundays and slept fewer hours. He took on an evening job moving crates at the docks—quiet, brutal work that blistered his hands and darkened his eyes.

Anya noticed the change, of course.

"You're chasing something," she said one night as they lay in bed, shoulder to shoulder. "You think if you work harder, the loss will go away."

Yusuf didn't answer.

She turned to face him. "Is it about the baby?"

"No," he said, finally. "It's about what comes next."

One evening in late May, he came home with dirt on his knees and a torn cuff on his shirt.

He handed Anya a folded envelope.

"What is it?"

"A name," he said. "One I'm giving away."

She opened it slowly. Inside were two sets of documents. One in Yusuf's name. The other in the name of *Joseph Halem*—his "younger brother."

Birthdate only two years apart. Parents' names identical. Port of origin slightly altered. Forged but convincing.

Anya looked up, her brow creased.

"This isn't your brother."

"No. But he's family."

Her hands trembled. "Yusuf... if they find out..."

"They won't."

"You could be deported. Jailed."

"I know."

She pressed the papers to her chest and sat down, her breath shaky.

"I thought we came here to become something better."

"We came here to survive," he said. "The better will come later."

When Kerem arrived three months later, it was under the name *Joseph Halem.*

Anya met him at the docks with Yusuf. He was thinner than Yusuf remembered, with eyes too old for his face and a limp he wouldn't explain. But when he smiled, it was like the war hadn't quite ruined everything.

Anya shook his hand but didn't speak much that day. Later, after Kerem had settled into the cot beside the stove, she sat across from Yusuf at their table, tea growing cold between them.

"You saved him," she said.

Yusuf stared into his cup. "I hope I didn't damn us both in the process."

The first Thursday after Kerem's arrival, Anya still lit the candle.

They ate simply: boiled eggs, flatbread, and lentils, a nod to the last meal Yusuf had shared with his cousin years before. Yusuf offered a toast—quiet and brief, in their native language.

"To paper sons," he said. "And to the real family they become."

Anya raised her cup, but her eyes held something distant—an awareness that some truths, no matter how noble, bend a little too far to stay whole.

That night, as she washed the dishes, she asked Yusuf softly, "When we have children again... will you tell them the truth?"

Yusuf didn't answer right away.

Then: "Only when they're ready to understand what survival costs."

In that moment, the seed of the family's first real secret was planted.

Not a lie, exactly. But a truth wrapped in silence, folded neatly into papers, passed down like an heirloom too fragile to explain.

And somewhere across the ocean, another war began to rise.

1942 – BROOKLYN, NEW YORK

The Valenko children grew up in two languages, but belonged to neither.

At home, the walls echoed with old words—soft consonants and rounded vowels soaked in history, used for lullabies, blessings, reprimands. "Eat." "Be careful." "Don't forget who you are." These words lived in the kitchen, between pots of cabbage stew and the steam of boiled linen. They clung to the corners of the tenement like soot.

But outside—on stoops and schoolyards—their names were shortened, their accents mocked, their prayers forgotten. Outside, they became *Joe* and *Ellie*, their laughter sharper, their English faster. At school, they practiced reciting the Pledge while slipping notes in cursive and playing hopscotch over the chalk outlines of what their parents had built with sweat and borrowed grace.

Their eldest, **Misha**, was the stillest of the three—a quiet boy with Yusuf's jaw and Anya's dark, thoughtful eyes. He read late into the night, books stacked like firewood beside his cot. War headlines curled across the front pages like smoke. He clipped articles and kept them in a shoebox: maps, telegrams, names of ships, enemy movements, casualty numbers.

One evening, Yusuf found him standing motionless at the kitchen window, his reflection ghosted against the night glass.

"You're too young to worry like that," Yusuf said, pouring tea.

"I'm not young anymore," Misha replied. He was seventeen. Already taller than his father, already looking past the windowsill as if it were a border he meant to cross.

Anya tried to keep the world away with soup and ceremony. She braided his hair tighter. Pressed talismans of garlic and dill into his coat pockets. But Misha carried the weight of a country he had never seen and another he didn't fully trust.

When he enlisted, he did not tell them until after the papers were signed.

Anya cried at the table, her hands pressed flat against the wood as if trying to hold the family in place.

Yusuf only asked, "Are you going because you believe in this war —or because you want to run from something?"

Misha didn't answer. He hugged his mother and left with his shoebox full of newspaper clippings and a single photograph—his parents on their wedding day, standing in a field with no fence behind them.

Helen, the middle child, did not cry when Misha left.

She was sixteen and already carrying fire in her voice, already speaking faster than her mother could follow. Helen wore her American identity like a coat two sizes too small—tight, hot, full of motion.

She corrected Anya's English in front of guests. Refused to wear braids past thirteen. Refused to learn the old recipes unless she could change them—add nutmeg where none belonged, switch chicken for beef, mix in flavors from Rosa's kitchen, from the Irish neighbors down the hall.

She wanted *new*. Not just new words, but new names, new maps, new music. She hummed jazz standards under her breath, bought magazines with movie stars on the cover, and once dared to wear lipstick out of the house—deep red, defiant.

Anya scrubbed her mouth raw when she came home.

At night, Helen wrote poems under the quilt her mother had sewn, hiding the notebook inside a shoebox marked *Helen Valenko, someday famous.* She dreamed of college. Of New York stages. Of a life where she could speak her truth—loudly, fluently, without translation.

Yusuf loved her fiercely but spoke to her like a man addressing thunder: with respect and caution.

"You are made of metal and smoke," he said once. "You will go far. But you will burn."

Helen kissed his forehead and said, "Then let me burn bright, Papa."

In the quiet between arguments and departures, Anya still lit the Thursday candle.

The children rarely noticed. But she did it anyway—faithfully, like the opening note of a song no one else remembered. Each week, she prepared a small meal with care, even when it was only her and Yusuf left at the table. She sprinkled dill over the bread, always. She watched the flame flicker, always.

One night, Yusuf sat beside her and took her hand.

"They don't speak our tongue anymore," he said.

"No," Anya replied. "But they still understand our silence."

He kissed her knuckles, rough from years of washing, of wringing, of planting things that sometimes bloomed and sometimes didn't.

And outside, somewhere far from Brooklyn, a train carried Misha into a war he couldn't pronounce, while Helen climbed a fire escape just to see the city lights and imagine a world that might finally, fully, be hers.

THANKSGIVING DAY, 1943 –
BROOKLYN, NEW YORK

By late November, the war was no longer something that happened far away. It bled into every corner of life—through black-and-white newspaper clippings pinned to kitchen walls, through ration books kept like prayer cards in pockets, through the hush that fell over dinner tables when someone mentioned a boy they used to know, now buried in a place no one could spell.

For the Valenkos, Thanksgiving arrived gray and damp, as if the season itself was unsure whether to lean toward mourning or celebration. The morning sky sat low over Brooklyn, the streets veiled in drizzle and factory smoke. Church bells rang hollow. On stoops and storefronts, flags hung limp with rain.

Inside their third-floor apartment, Anya stirred a pot of broth that would have been soup if the ration book allowed it. The chicken she had managed to buy was small, pale, more bone than bird. She had brined it overnight in vinegar and onion peel, hoping to coax out flavor. The potatoes were spotted. The carrots shriveled. Still, she washed and peeled with the same diligence as she had twenty years before.

There had always been hunger. But this was a different kind.

It was the hunger of waiting. Of not knowing. Of watching the door.

The apartment was quiet except for the soft hum of the radio, where a newscaster droned about troop movements in France and the promise of a long winter. Anya let his voice wash over her like background noise—too familiar now to be alarming.

Helen sat at the kitchen table, reading the same page of a novel for the third time. Her lipstick—worn out of habit now—was a muted shade of plum, her curls pinned back with silver clips. She had grown into herself in the years since Misha left, but there was a brittleness to her confidence now, like thin ice under a polished surface. She looked grown, but she felt undone.

"It smells like something," she said, not looking up from the book.

Anya stirred the broth. "Like what?"

"Not home," Helen said. "But close."

Anya didn't reply.

She pulled a bread loaf from the oven—flat, dense, studded with herbs from the windowsill. The scent rose warmly, filling the small room. It was a poor imitation of the loaves she used to bake in the village, but it was made with care. Intention. Ritual.

Rosa had stopped by earlier with a pie crust filled with something resembling apples—though both women had laughed and admitted neither was certain what fruit had actually gone into it. They had shared tea, complained about meat prices, compared the weight under their eyes. Then Rosa kissed Anya's cheek and whispered, "Your boy will come home. He's too stubborn not to."

Anya had smiled, but her heart did not agree.

She had not heard from Misha in over six weeks. Letters had come at first—short, careful, laced with optimism—but they had slowed. Then stopped. The last one had mentioned fog and fatigue and a sergeant who snored through air raids.

Yusuf entered then, carrying a sack of kindling, his coat soaked through from the walk back from the factory. Though he now worked fewer hours, the effort still bent his shoulders in ways that seemed permanent. His knuckles were cracked. His boots leaked. But he tried not to bring the heaviness home. It was a losing battle.

He kissed Anya's forehead as he passed, then nodded toward the stove.

"You made a feast," he said.

"I made what I could."

He said nothing more. He stripped off his coat, hung it near the radiator, and sat at the table beside Helen, his eyes lingering a beat too long on the empty chair where Misha once sat.

They set the table just after dusk.

Two candles. One for light. One for him.

Anya laid the cloth flat, smoothing the creases with both hands. She unfolded the cloth napkins she had sewn from remnants of flour sacks. She placed the mismatched plates with a kind of reverence, pausing over the fourth one. It felt both indulgent and necessary to set it.

"This is strange," Helen said, looking at the extra plate.

"No," Anya replied. "It is tradition."

"Tradition is strange."

Yusuf shot her a look, but it lacked heat. He had long ago stopped trying to argue Helen out of her sharpness. Instead, he reached for her hand.

"Your brother's still with us," he said. "Even if his food gets cold."

Helen didn't argue. But she didn't take his hand, either.

They sat. They bowed their heads.

Yusuf spoke in the old language, words slow and steady. A blessing for health, for warmth, for the chance to be together. A prayer for those far from home. A whisper to the ancestors, to the earth, to whatever force still kept bones knitted and breath moving.

Anya opened her eyes at the end of it and found herself staring at Misha's chair.

She did not weep.

They ate slowly. Sparingly. Bread dipped in broth, chicken passed carefully. The conversation danced around the war—never direct, never detailed. It was easier to speak of Helen's latest poem, of the Polish grocer's new baby, of the way the roof in the tenement next door had finally collapsed.

Just as Anya reached for the pie, there was a knock at the door.

Not loud. But firm.

Helen stood, hesitating a moment before opening it.

A man in a gray overcoat stood in the hallway, shoulders hunched, hat pulled low. He smelled of damp wool and ink. His gloved hand held a single envelope—long, pale yellow, the color of sour milk.

He did not meet her eyes.

"Telegram," he said, placing it in her palm.

She closed the door slowly.

The room went silent.

Anya stood before Helen could even speak. Her hand reached, not trembling, but deliberate.

The envelope was marked: *War Department. Official Communication.*

Anya opened it without ceremony. No hesitation. Her eyes moved across the page once. Then again.

"He's alive," she said. Her voice did not break.

Helen gasped. Yusuf exhaled a breath that had been hiding in his chest for weeks.

"France," Anya continued. "Injured. Left leg. But alive."

She folded the telegram and held it to her chest like scripture.

Yusuf rose, placed a hand on her back.

Helen sat heavily, pie untouched in front of her.

"Wounded," she said softly. "That means he's seen things."

Anya nodded. "We all have."

Later, they lit a third candle.

For his leg. For his return. For whatever he would be when he came back.

Anya went to the bedroom and brought out a small box—tied with twine, wrapped in brown paper. Inside was Misha's first letter from overseas. He had included a photograph: three soldiers on a rooftop, arms slung around each other, smiling into the wind.

Anya placed the photo at the center of the table.

The candles flickered. Outside, footsteps echoed down the alley. A car backfired. Music played faintly from a neighbor's record player —a scratchy waltz, off-tempo, mournful.

Inside, the apartment was full of the scent of herbs and starch and smoke.

The feast continued.

And though their son was far away, and forever changed, there was bread. There was broth. There was breath.

In this, they found their own way to be thankful.

Not for the war. Not for the wound.

But for the fact that, somewhere across the ocean, **Misha was still breathing**.

And as long as he breathed, they would leave a place at the table.

THANKSGIVING DAY, 1946 –
BROOKLYN, NEW YORK

The war was over, but the house did not feel victorious.

It was quieter, certainly. Misha had come home with a cane and a changed voice, his gaze always just past people, as if looking for something that wasn't there. He spent long hours by the window, smoking in silence, the French locket he brought back clinking quietly against the radiator. He had survived—but survival was not the same as return.

Helen, on the other hand, came back changed in another way: dressed in a pale blue suit and a ring on her finger.

His name was **Frank Delaney**, and he smelled like shaving cream and coffee and the faint trace of streetcar grease. He had a good jaw, a better grin, and the kind of confidence that sat too comfortably in other people's kitchens. He worked in the transit union, voted Democrat, said *"ma'am"* to Anya and called Yusuf *"sir"* the first time they met. It didn't help.

He was **Irish-American**. Brooklyn born. Catholic. Fast-talking.

And Helen had married him on a Monday without telling anyone.

The letter announcing it arrived four days before Thanksgiving—

no invitation, just a note, folded twice, with Helen's unmistakable looping script.

Anya read it once. Then again. Then set it on the counter and continued washing carrots, the water running longer than necessary.

That Thanksgiving, the air in the Valenko apartment was taut and over-seasoned. The table was set, as always, with care: mismatched china, starched napkins, bread folded into soft little knots, the herbs from Anya's tin pail still clinging to life near the window. A roast duck sizzled in the oven, filling the apartment with warmth and ritual.

Helen arrived late.

Her coat was red. Her lips, too. She stepped into the kitchen with a smile too bright to be natural.

Frank followed behind, balancing a bakery pie box in his hands. He glanced around the small apartment with polite curiosity, nodding toward the hallway and the framed embroidery that read *"To remember is to honor."* He had never seen a home like this.

"Thank you for having us," he said, extending the pie. "Pumpkin. From Gino's on Seventh."

Yusuf took it without comment.

Helen removed her coat slowly, revealing the pale blue of her dress—the same one from the wedding photo they had not received.

"You look older," Anya said.

Helen smiled faintly. "Marriage does that."

Misha said nothing, just flicked his cigarette into the sink and left the room.

They sat, awkwardly, around the table.

Anya lit the candle. Yusuf gave the blessing, his words sharper than usual, each syllable clipped like a warning. Helen bowed her head but did not close her eyes.

The meal began.

Frank tried. He asked about Yusuf's work. Mentioned politics. Told a story about a trolley derailment in Queens, full of humor, sharp timing, a good punchline. But it fell flat. Anya offered him more potatoes without speaking. Misha ate like he was somewhere else.

Helen pushed food around her plate.

At one point, she reached for the bread and said, "Frank's mother makes soda bread every Sunday."

Anya looked up. "Does she bake with her mother's hands, too?"

Frank's smile faltered.

Yusuf cleared his throat. "And what will your children learn? Which table will they sit at?"

Helen straightened in her chair. "Whichever one loves them."

Silence.

Even the duck seemed to stop steaming.

After the meal, Helen stood at the sink, her hands submerged in lukewarm water. Anya dried. Neither looked at the other.

"You didn't tell us," Anya said.

"I didn't need permission."

"No. You needed courage."

Helen turned, the towel dropping into the sink.

"You taught me to speak. To fight. To want. And now that I do, you want me quiet."

"I want you to belong."

"I do belong. Just not the way you dreamed."

Anya reached for the bread knife, wiped it clean, then set it down with care.

"He's not of us."

"No," Helen said softly. "But I am. And that has to be enough."

Later, after the dishes were stacked and the tea was cold, Misha approached Helen as she tied her scarf.

"He seems kind," he said quietly. "But I don't know how to place him."

"You don't have to," Helen said. "You just have to let me place myself."

He nodded. "Mama won't forget. You know that?"

"She doesn't have to. I just hope she remembers more than the wound."

He kissed her cheek before she left.

That night, after Frank and Helen walked back into the city fog, Anya stood in the doorway of the kitchen, arms crossed, watching the wind tug at the curtains. The candle had burned low.

Yusuf came behind her, placed a hand on her shoulder.

"She married someone who will stay," he said.

"I know."

"She will always speak in two tongues."

"I know."

"She is still ours."

Anya nodded.

"I know," she whispered. "But knowing doesn't make it easier."

And in the flickering light of a half-empty table, the meaning of Thanksgiving shifted again—no longer just a tether to the past, but a fragile truce between generations, between identities, between love and disappointment.

Between staying and going.

AUTUMN, 1945 – BROOKLYN, NEW YORK

The war ended with bells.

Church bells. Factory whistles. Car horns, shouted headlines, flags pulled from dusty closets and waved like old dreams. On the streets, people danced and wept and kissed strangers without apology. Wine was poured from chipped teacups. Radios blared big band music as if joy could be choreographed. *Victory*, they called it, though few knew what they had actually won.

Inside the Valenko apartment, Yusuf said nothing.

He sat at the kitchen table with his coat still on, the newspaper folded neatly before him. Misha had read the headline aloud that morning—*Germany Surrenders*, followed by dates and declarations, names of generals and treaties and promises of peace. He had smiled when he read it. But Yusuf had only nodded and returned to his tea.

He had waited years for this moment. But now that it had arrived, it felt shapeless. Like standing at the edge of a long field, only to find it barren.

In the weeks that followed, the apartment filled with signs of life returning. Misha got work delivering supplies to the city's hospitals. He still limped, but less. Helen visited with Frank on Sundays, bringing bags of oranges and sharp-tongued stories from the outer boroughs. She always arrived laughing, left tense. She had learned to navigate the gap between her two homes, but not to close it.

Anya, for her part, returned to rhythm. Laundry. Loaves. Tea and small talk. But her eyes searched Yusuf's face more often now, as if studying a map she could no longer read.

He was quieter in a new way.

Before, his silence had been full of focus—a kind of presence held between breaths. Now it was absence disguised as patience. He took long walks without telling her where. He sat by the radio but didn't listen. He began writing things down—lists, memories, phrases from the old language—and hiding them in drawers.

Sometimes she caught him staring at the window long after the sun had gone. Watching shadows, or ghosts.

It was in October, just after the leaves turned, that Anya found the first burned letter.

She had been sweeping the hallway when she noticed a curl of ash near the stove, finer than the kind that came from firewood. Not gray. Charred. Paper.

She knelt, brushed her fingers through it.

There were more pieces beneath the grate—blackened edges, bits of envelope. She lifted one and read a single unburned word: **Kerem.**

Her heart stalled.

That night, she asked Yusuf directly.

"Are you writing to him again?"

He looked up from his tea.

"I was never not writing."

"Then why burn them?"

He didn't answer.

She sat across from him, folding her hands into her lap. "You promised."

"I kept the promise."

"To him or to me?"

Yusuf's jaw tensed. He rose, crossed to the cupboard, and

retrieved a small tin box. Inside were half-burned pages, folded tightly, scorched at the edges like the remnants of a sacred book.

He set it on the table between them.

"Not everything belongs to memory," he said. "Some things must die to stay buried."

The truth was: he had not heard from Kerem in over a year. The last letter had arrived thin, written in a rushed hand, full of references to men and movements Yusuf no longer understood. There were rumors. The name **Joseph Halem** had surfaced in the wrong mouths. The war had made many things possible, but peace—true peace—did not know how to find men like them.

And so Yusuf wrote back. And burned what he wrote. Each letter a confession he couldn't afford to send.

He wrote of the first forged document. Of the night he paid a man to turn paper into blood. Of the dreams he still had—Kerem running barefoot through a train yard, one shoe in hand, the other foot bleeding. He wrote of guilt. Of names. Of not knowing what survival had cost until it came stamped with victory.

On the last Thursday of November, Anya still lit the candle.

Misha brought a bottle of wine and a loaf of bakery bread—soft, but flavorless. Helen brought a record, jazz with scratchy horns. Frank did not come. He had to work, she said. Or maybe he didn't. She didn't offer more.

They ate duck again, though it was drier than usual. Yusuf said little. When Misha made a joke about victory and leftovers, his father only nodded.

The radio played low in the corner. Outside, children shouted beneath fire escapes. Someone launched a firecracker early. It fizzled, then cracked like a gunshot.

Yusuf flinched.

Anya touched his hand. "The war is over."

He didn't look at her.

"Not for everyone," he said.

That night, when the children had gone and the apartment was dim with coals and leftover heat, Anya found the tin box gone from its place.

Yusuf sat by the window, a shawl across his lap, staring out at the smoke drifting from chimneys. She joined him but didn't speak.

In his lap was a photograph—faded and cracked, from before the war. Before America. Two boys, shoulder to shoulder, one holding a book, the other with a defiant smirk. She hadn't seen it in years.

She reached for it. He didn't pull away.

"We were seventeen," he said. "He taught me how to steal plums from the orchard. I taught him how to read poetry."

"And now?"

Yusuf folded the photo back into the book on his knees.

"Now I don't know if he's dead. Or if I just buried him so well I can no longer tell the difference."

In the morning, ash clung to the stovetop again.

Anya swept it away without a word.

And somewhere between the silence and the smoke, the war carved one more line into the heart of their home—not loud, not sudden, but lasting.

Victory had come. But it had not made them whole.

It had only made them quiet.

AUTUMN, 1948 – QUEENS, NEW YORK

They said it was the American dream. A house. A yard. A door you could lock from the inside. A deed with your name on it—spelled correctly or not.

Yusuf didn't speak when they signed the papers, but his hand trembled as he pressed the pen to the page. His name had changed twice since stepping onto Ellis Island, but this one—this last version—was the one that would be carved into a mailbox on Elm Street.

Anya wore her best blouse, the one with the blue embroidery near the cuffs. Her hair was pinned neatly, her shoes polished. But inside, her chest felt strange—tight, expectant, like she was waiting for something to go wrong. Still, she smiled when the realtor handed over the key: a simple piece of metal with chipped teeth and promise baked into its dull shine.

They moved in on a Wednesday. It was raining. Helen and Misha helped carry boxes up the front steps while Anya stood in the living room, looking out through the wide front window onto a block lined with identical shrubs and postwar hope.

"This is it?" Helen asked, her voice caught between wonder and disbelief. "It looks like Monopoly."

Misha laughed and shook water from his coat. "Just wait. Mama will make it smell like home by sundown."

She did.

She unpacked her clay herb pots and placed them on the sill. She folded linens into the new drawers and lined the pantry with brown paper before filling it. She placed the wedding photograph of her and Yusuf—aged and grain-specked—on the mantel above the unused fireplace. And above that, she tacked the cross-stitch that had followed them through tenements and apartments and borrowed rooms:

To remember is to honor.

The house had three bedrooms. A real kitchen. A stairwell that creaked with honesty. The radiator hissed like an old friend. There was a fig tree out back that hadn't borne fruit in years, but Yusuf swore he could coax it into giving.

They had arrived. At last.

But not completely.

That Thanksgiving was the first one in the new house. Anya began preparing days in advance, her hands moving with both excitement and a kind of private dread. New walls. New air. But memory still clung to her ribs like old grief.

She unpacked the good dishes—gifts from Rosa years ago, now chipped at the corners but still lovely. She ironed the tablecloth twice. Yusuf scrubbed the stoop and trimmed the hedges with the same solemnity he once used to clean tombstones. Misha brought fresh apples from a market run by a veteran who called him *sir*. Helen offered to help but arrived late, carrying an armful of fabric scraps and a story about a blocked train line that no one fully believed.

Frank did not come.

They had separated that summer—quietly, without lawyers or ceremony. He had returned to his mother's house in Bay Ridge. Helen had stayed in a walk-up with a part-time roommate and three typewriters, one of which worked. She didn't speak of it much. Only once had she said to Anya, while helping cut vegetables, *"Some men love women. Others love certainty. He needed more of the second."*

Now she arrived with lipstick slightly smudged and a pie that had collapsed slightly in the center. "It's abstract," she said. "Like modern art."

Dinner was bigger than before. Not extravagant, but deliberate. There were guests—neighbors from two doors down. A quiet couple from Romania with a baby that blinked solemnly through the entire meal. There was laughter, cautious and shared like bread. Music from the record player. The smell of rosemary and cloves rising through the air.

But the house did not echo yet. It was still learning how to hold their voices. Still unfamiliar.

Yusuf carved the bird with a precision that felt reverent. Misha poured the wine. Helen made a toast.

"To the house," she said, glass raised, "and to all the ghosts who won't fit inside it."

The room fell still, then slowly lifted again with laughter.

Later, as the guests trickled out and the plates sat crusted and empty in the sink, Anya stood at the threshold of the hallway, watching Yusuf as he stoked the fire for the first time. He had waited all evening. Now, with the house dim and the children upstairs, he knelt, feeding the match into the stacked wood with a slowness that made it feel sacred.

Flame caught. Shadows leapt.

He sat back on his heels, watching.

Anya joined him.

"Does it feel like home?" she asked.

"No," he said honestly. "Not yet."

She nodded.

"I keep thinking of the first apartment," she whispered. "The stove we had to kick. The bread that stuck to the pan. The bed that cried louder than the baby ever did."

"I miss the noise," he said.

"This is better."

He nodded. "It is."

But still—he reached into his coat pocket and pulled out something folded: an old letter, yellowed and soft at the edges. He didn't read it. Just held it. Then fed it gently into the fire.

They watched it curl and vanish.

Upstairs, Helen lay awake in the guest room, staring at the ceiling. Misha snored softly in the room across the hall. The baby next door wailed once and was quickly soothed. The house listened. It held every sound.

The fig tree outside shivered in the wind.

And in the quiet, where old worlds had ended and new ones were still taking shape, Thanksgiving settled again—not a celebration, but a marker.

Not wholeness. Not yet.

But shelter.

And space.

And a table set with both memory and hope.

THANKSGIVING DAY, 1965 – QUEENS, NEW YORK

By the time the youngest Valenko grandchild turned thirteen, the house on Elm Street no longer smelled like old bread and rosemary.

It smelled like *plastic*. Like hairspray. Like frozen pie crusts and canned yams and television static humming through the walls. It smelled like something becoming other than what it had been—and no one knew quite how to say so without sounding ungrateful.

The dining room had been painted lemon yellow the year before. The wallpaper with the faded tulips had been peeled away in strips, and with it went something else—something unsayable. The old table was still there, but its edges had dulled with years of elbows and disagreements. Anya's sewing machine now lived beneath a plastic cover. Yusuf's hands trembled when he tried to thread a needle.

And the television—new, expensive, always on—sat like a shrine in the living room, pulling attention away from candles and conversation and toward black-and-white newsreels of a country unraveling.

The children spoke quickly now, like they were racing toward something. They interrupted. They argued. They did not bow their heads when the blessing was given.

One boy wore a denim jacket with a peace sign scrawled across the back in permanent marker. Another girl, barely sixteen, wore a black armband in protest of the war and refused to eat turkey "while napalm fell on villages."

Anya didn't understand half of what they said, and the half she did understand, she didn't like.

Helen's daughter, **Marianne**, had stopped wearing dresses. She called Yusuf *"Grandpa Joe"* even though Anya had never once spoken that name aloud in her life. The boy—**Sam**—chewed gum at the table and called Thanksgiving *"a colonialist myth."*

When Anya asked him what he meant, he rolled his eyes and said, *"It's just a story white people made up to feel better about genocide."*

"But you are not white," Anya said, her voice sharper than she meant.

He shrugged. "Depends who's asking."

Yusuf said nothing.

The tension built slowly, like heat under a sealed lid.

The grandchildren debated Vietnam as if it were a dinner party game. Misha—who still walked with a limp, though he never mentioned it—sat quietly, gripping his fork until his knuckles blanched.

"They're drafting children," one girl snapped.

"They're not children once they hold a rifle," Misha muttered.

Helen interjected, "They are *someone's* children."

"No one's sending your children," Misha said, too quickly.

And just like that, the air split.

Helen stiffened. Sam stood abruptly, muttering something about the bathroom but not returning. Marianne followed.

After the meal, the kitchen was too quiet. The dishes sat soaking in lukewarm water. Helen stood at the window, arms folded, watching the neighbors' boy toss a football across their dead lawn.

"They don't understand," she said.

"No," Anya replied. "But they feel very sure."

Helen turned. "Did we sound like that? Once?"

Anya's smile was sad. "You did. You still do."

Helen took a breath, then lowered herself onto the stool by the counter. "It's harder now. Everything is louder."

"Louder is not the same as stronger."

Helen nodded. "They're angry. All the time. They want to fix everything, but they hate everything too."

"They are Americans," Anya said quietly. "Fully."

Yusuf remained at the table, staring out the window, untouched pie in front of him. He had barely spoken during dinner. The arguments had moved around him like waves around a stone.

He took the photo of his mother from the bookshelf and placed it beside the candle. A quiet gesture. An offering. No one noticed.

That night, when the guests had left and the television was finally off, Anya stood in the hallway, watching her home breathe.

It still held the same bones. But something had shifted.

The children didn't want the recipes anymore. They didn't want the language. They didn't even want the stories.

"They want fire," she whispered to Yusuf.

"They were born into it," he said.

She took his hand, brittle now but familiar. They stood there a long time, listening to the radiator hiss and the wind press against the windows.

This Thanksgiving had been larger. Louder. But not warmer.

Tradition, it seemed, could not always stretch far enough to cover what grew wild in its shadow.

LATE AUTUMN, 1967 – QUEENS, NEW YORK

Helen came home with two children, a suitcase, and the look of someone who had stopped asking for directions a long time ago.

There was no ceremony to her arrival. No announcement, no apology. Just the scrape of the key in the front door, the muted thud of boots against the hallway tile, and the way she stood in the doorway as if she wasn't sure whether to call it entering or returning.

Anya was in the kitchen, rinsing dill under cold water, the sink filling slowly beside her. She knew it was Helen by the silence—her daughter's silences always came first, before footsteps or breath, shaped like a question that dared not be asked.

She turned off the faucet, dried her hands, and said, without turning around, "You came."

"I didn't know where else to go."

"Then this is the right place."

That was all.

No embrace. No scolding. Only the quiet surrender of a woman who knew the cost of distance and the limits of pride.

The children entered a moment later, blinking up at the hallway like it was too narrow to hold them. **Marianne**, twelve, carried a small radio and a book she didn't look up from. Her hair was pulled tight at the scalp, too adult for her face. **Sam**, nine, trailed behind with a backpack and a green plastic dinosaur, which he clutched like a talisman.

They were not shy, not rude, but something else—*strangers in the shape of family.* They greeted Anya with polite nods and half-smiles, but no hugs. No stories. They walked into the house as if passing through it.

Anya offered tea. Marianne declined. Sam shrugged. Helen accepted but didn't drink.

Yusuf came in from the back porch, wiping paint off his hands. He stopped in the doorway, his eyes lingering on Helen's coat, her hands, the fine new lines around her mouth. Then he looked at the children —his grandchildren—and for a moment something flickered across his face: not quite recognition, not quite welcome.

"I made up the spare room," he said.

Helen nodded. "Thank you."

He left without another word.

That night, the house creaked under old memories and new tension. The radiator clanked like it was clearing its throat. Marianne complained about the blankets being "too heavy." Sam fell asleep with the light on.

Helen stayed up late, alone at the kitchen table, drinking tea that had long gone cold. The walls around her held pictures of a life she had tried, for years, to leave behind. Embroidered prayers. Faded photos. A portrait of herself at seventeen in a handmade dress, caught in sepia between rebellion and obedience.

Anya joined her just after midnight, wearing her housecoat and carrying a tin of dry cookies she hadn't served. She sat down across from her daughter.

"You were always restless," she said.

Helen stared at the rim of her mug. "I thought I could outrun certain things."

"And now?"

"I realize I packed them with me."

They sat in silence, the clock ticking on the stove.

"I didn't want to raise them like this," Helen said finally. "I didn't want to bring them here and pretend this house can fix what I broke."

"It doesn't need to fix," Anya said. "Only hold."

Helen swallowed hard. "They don't even speak the language."

"Neither do you, anymore."

A beat passed. Then they both smiled. Tired. Sad. True.

Thanksgiving came three days later.

It had once been a proud, sprawling event—extra chairs, laughter down the hallway, the smell of sage and garlic so thick it clung to your clothes until Tuesday. But this year, it was quieter. Smaller. A room rearranged for absences.

Misha came early, with his usual cranberry sauce and a new limp he didn't explain. He kissed Anya on the cheek, clapped Yusuf on the shoulder, and looked at Helen for a long time before saying simply, "You made it."

"Barely," she replied.

He nodded, and they both left it there.

The dinner was strained from the start.

Sam asked if there would be TV after. Marianne complained about the stuffing. Helen hovered between trying to parent and trying not to fail in front of her own.

Yusuf said little. He watched, fork in hand, as generations collided across the table. Anya, ever the mediator, offered seconds and soft words, but the tension floated like steam above every plate.

When Helen began to speak about her job search, Marianne rolled her eyes.

"I don't want to live here forever," she said, stabbing her peas.

"You're not," Helen replied. "This is just temporary."

"Until when?" Sam asked.

Helen didn't answer.

Anya cleared the plates early. She couldn't stand the scraping of utensils on porcelain any longer.

Later, after the children had gone upstairs and Yusuf had turned on the radio to drown out the quiet, Anya and Helen washed the dishes together.

It was the first time they had stood side by side like that in years— hands working in rhythm, hip to hip, elbows occasionally bumping.

"I wasn't a good wife," Helen said suddenly.

Anya didn't flinch.

"You were a wife."

"I don't know if I'm a good mother."

Anya turned off the tap, drying her hands slowly.

"Are they warm at night?"

"Yes."

"Do they know you love them?"

Helen hesitated. "I try."

"Then you are enough."

Helen's hands began to shake. Water dripped from her wrists like baptism.

"I thought I was building something different than you did."

"You did," Anya said. "But you are still part of this house. And this house remembers."

Later that night, Helen stood in the doorway of the guest room, watching her children sleep.

Marianne's limbs were tangled in sheets, her brow furrowed even in dreams. Sam clutched the plastic dinosaur to his chest like it held secrets.

Helen leaned against the frame, arms crossed.

Yusuf passed behind her, pausing.

"She reminds me of you," he said quietly, nodding toward Marianne.

Helen smiled. "That's not a comfort."

"It will be. In time."

She looked up at him, her eyes full.

"Do you think I'll be okay?"

"No," he said. "But you'll keep going."

Thanksgiving ended not with a toast or a fire or the telling of old stories.

It ended with two women standing at the sink, side by side. With a man watching his daughter become real to him again, even in her wreckage. With children upstairs dreaming in half-familiar beds. With old furniture and older fears.

And with one truth standing quietly in the middle of the house:

That sometimes, return isn't about finding home again—

But about letting it hold you until you can rebuild.

WINTER, 1969 – QUEENS, NEW YORK

Anya had begun to forget things.

Small things, at first—a pan left on the stove, a sentence left unfinished, a name left waiting in the hallway of her mind. She still moved with purpose, still peeled potatoes with the same quiet rhythm, still lit a candle on Thursday evenings. But now she sometimes lit two. Or forgot she had done it at all.

The family chalked it up to age, to exhaustion, to too many decades in a body that had absorbed grief like rain into stone. But it was more than that. Something inside her was coming undone, like thread slipping from a needle.

And yet, there were moments—**bright**, startling moments—when her voice returned sharp, full of color, brimming with stories no one remembered asking for but now couldn't bear to interrupt.

Leah listened.

Leah was fifteen and soft around the edges, all eyes and questions. She was Helen's youngest, the quiet one, the reader, the one who stayed late after dinners and watched Anya's hands instead of the television.

She had never known the tenement, had never seen her grandfather's hands before the tremors began. She didn't speak the old language, not really, but she carried its cadence in the way she listened.

She was the only one who didn't correct Anya when she slipped into phrases from before.

They sat together in the sunroom on Sunday afternoons, Anya wrapped in a shawl that had once belonged to her sister, Leah curled beside her with a notebook she rarely dared to open.

Sometimes Anya would reach for the air in front of her, as if brushing invisible curtains aside.

"Your grandfather," she said one day, "he once carried a pig's head down Grand Street in his bare hands. No bag. Blood on his coat. He looked like God's butcher."

Leah blinked. "Was it for a holiday?"

Anya laughed softly, a rusted sound. "No. Just hunger."

Another time, Anya pointed to the fig tree outside—bare, brittle, forgotten.

"Did I ever tell you about Marseille?" she asked.

"No," Leah whispered, though she had heard the city's name in fragments, always like a warning.

"There was a man," Anya said. "Or a ghost. Or both. He sent letters. Your grandfather burned them, but not before I read them."

"Who was he?"

Anya's eyes grew glassy. "He was Yusuf's brother. But not really. He came with a name that wasn't his. Or maybe it was. Sometimes I don't remember who we were before we became who we had to be."

The stories came in fits and starts. Half-formed memories. Names mispronounced. A wedding that may never have happened. A night in a church basement, hiding beneath pews while snow swallowed the city whole. A recipe from her mother, once written down, now recited in rhyme:

"Two parts flour, one part grief.

A pinch of salt, to hold belief.
Boil when frightened. Serve with tears."

Leah scribbled it down in her notebook, unsure if it was a poem, a recipe, or both.

No one else sat with Anya like that.

Helen was too busy, always working or folding laundry or trying to stretch time like dough over too many responsibilities. Marianne was gone—college, protests, long phone calls from cities far away. Sam had retreated into headphones and half-smiles.

Even Yusuf had grown more distant, though he still made her tea and wrapped her feet in wool socks when she forgot how to do it herself.

But it was Leah who listened.

Leah who remembered.

Leah who knew that the stories, even in their fragmentary, crumbling form, were **inheritance**.

One evening, as wind howled through the eaves and the fig tree scratched against the window like it wanted to be let inside, Anya reached for Leah's hand and held it, fragile and cool.

"You must ask questions," she said. "Before I forget the answers."

Leah nodded, tears she didn't understand prickling behind her eyes.

"Who were we?" she asked.

Anya looked into the middle distance, past the walls, past the present.

"We were hungry. And holy. And afraid. We were paper sons and barefoot daughters. We were fire under water. And we are still here."

She paused.

"But I won't be for long."

That night, Leah copied every word she could remember into her notebook. She didn't edit. Didn't rearrange. Just let the words spill, crooked and spellbound. Her handwriting looked like it belonged to someone older.

When Helen peeked in on her later, Leah closed the notebook and said, "Did Grandma ever tell you about Marseille?"

Helen stared. "No. Why?"

"No reason," Leah said. "Just... she remembers it sometimes."

Helen left the room quietly.

Downstairs, Anya slept in her chair, the candle burned low beside her.

Her lips moved in sleep, whispering to someone not in the room. Her hands curled gently over her lap, palms open, as if she were holding something that could not be seen.

The house breathed around her.

And upstairs, Leah kept writing—

catching the voices of the past

before they vanished like steam

off a forgotten cup of tea.

EARLY SPRING, 1970 – NEW YORK CITY

Yusuf Halem died without ceremony.

No vigil. No last words. No reaching for hands or dramatic sighs. Just a quiet breath in the early hours of a Tuesday morning, alone in a hospital room that smelled like bleach and lavender soap and the slow exhale of old machines.

The nurse said he had smiled in his sleep.

No one knew at what. Or who.

Anya had fallen asleep beside him in the chair, her shawl tucked around her knees, her head resting against the wall. She woke to silence—**the kind of silence that rearranges the air**. Not empty, but *after*. A silence that knew something sacred had just left.

She didn't cry.

Instead, she stood, smoothed his blanket, and kissed his forehead like she had a thousand times before—when he left for work, when he returned, when he sat wordless at the table while a war played out in his eyes.

Then she whispered, "Go, then. But not far."

They buried Yusuf three days later.

It rained—not the kind of storm that floods grief loose, but a slow, hesitant drizzle, like the sky was still deciding whether to mourn. The cemetery was quiet. Modest stones. Sparse trees. Rows and rows of names trying to outlive time.

The family came as they always did—fragmented, distracted, dressed in shades of obligation.

Misha gave the eulogy. He spoke plainly. Of hard work. Of loyalty. Of a man who said little and meant more.

Helen stood at the back, Marianne beside her, neither wearing black. Leah clutched her notebook but didn't open it. Sam lit a cigarette too close to the gate.

Anya stood alone, without umbrella or coat, her hand resting on Yusuf's closed box of letters.

They found it in the closet, three days before the funeral.

It was old, cedar-lined, and locked.

Inside:

• A **folded photograph**—two boys on a dirt road, one of them clearly Yusuf, the other labeled *Kerem* in Yusuf's careful script.

• **Forged documents**—passports, identity forms, written in a mix of languages, ink smudged with time.

• A small **tobacco tin** filled with **burned fragments of letters**, one barely legible: *Tell them I was never brave, only necessary.*

• A **worn map** of a country that no longer existed.

• And a **single note**, written in Yusuf's unmistakable hand:
"I gave away pieces of myself so you could inherit something whole.
Tell the truth gently.
Not all roots grow straight."

The box changed things.

It cracked open a secret the family had never had words for. One they had only circled, felt beneath floorboards, glimpsed in the shadows of Anya's eyes or Yusuf's refusals to speak.

Misha refused to talk about it. "It doesn't matter," he said. "The past doesn't need a spotlight. It needs rest."

Helen disagreed. "You can't build a life on someone else's name and call it truth."

They fought, once, in the kitchen, voices raised over roast potatoes and too much wine.

"Everything we are is built on a lie!" Helen said.

"No," Anya said quietly, from the doorway. "Everything we are is built on *a choice*. And choice is heavier than truth."

The room fell still.

Leah sat with the box for hours. Not reading. Just being near it.

She copied Yusuf's final note into her notebook in three languages—English, phonetic Russian, and a half-invented version of what she imagined he might have spoken to his cousin on the docks of Marseille, on the edge of a war, beneath a name that wasn't quite his.

She placed a sprig of dried dill between the pages.

The following Thursday, Anya didn't light a candle.

She set the table, made the broth, folded the bread—but when Leah asked where the candle was, Anya shook her head.

"His silence was sacred," she said. "And he's keeping it still."

That night, Anya sat alone in the living room, Yusuf's coat draped over the back of his chair. The radio played something slow, something with strings. Rain patted softly against the window.

Leah stood in the hallway, watching, unsure whether to go in.

"Come," Anya said.

Leah did.

"Tell me a story," Anya said.

"But I don't know any," Leah whispered.

"Yes," Anya said. "You do. I gave them to you."

So Leah began.

She told Yusuf's story.

But she told it gently.

And Anya closed her eyes—not in grief, but in relief.

Because in that moment,
the silence was not an absence.
It was a **transfer.**
A passing.
A trust.

THANKSGIVING DAY, 1973 – QUEENS, NEW YORK

There was no candle that year.

No music. No soft voice humming over broth. No hands folding napkins into birds. No scent of fresh dill cut from the windowsill—only dust and silence and a strange sense of having arrived somewhere without remembering the journey.

Anya had been gone for nine months.

Her absence did not echo through the house; it hovered. It pressed against the windows, lingered in the corners of rooms where her footsteps once knew the floor. It waited at the table, beside the sink, at the top of the stairs—quiet, insistent, shapeless.

Grief did not wail in this house. It simply settled.

They gathered, as they had promised they would, though the promise had been spoken softly at her funeral, half-swallowed between obligations and casseroles.

Misha came first, alone, older than he had ever allowed himself to be. His hair was thinning. His coat too big. He brought wine but no pie.

Helen arrived two hours later with Marianne and Sam in tow. Marianne had become a teacher, engaged to someone none of them had met. Sam, now in college, smoked menthols on the porch and didn't bother hiding the smell.

No one offered to cook.

No one asked for help.

The turkey came pre-cooked from a market on Northern Boulevard.

The stuffing was box-mix. The cranberry sauce still bore the ridges of the can.

The meal was awkward in the way only shared history can be— heavy with implication, sagging with things unsaid.

They ate in silence for the first fifteen minutes.

Then, small talk.

Sam spoke about campus protests. Marianne mentioned wedding venues. Misha said something about traffic, about taxes, about how the roof needed patching.

Helen sat stiffly, folding her napkin again and again in her lap like a child punished in church.

Leah, now in her twenties, was the only one who looked like she remembered what this meal had once meant. She picked at her food. Her eyes wandered the room, stopping often on the empty chair at the head of the table.

"She would have hated this," she said finally.

Everyone looked up.

Helen sighed. "She would've hated the boxed stuffing."

"No," Leah said. "She would've hated *us*, like this. Going through the motions. Forgetting how to mean it."

Misha cleared his throat. "People grieve differently."

"Grief isn't what this is," Leah replied. "This is forgetting on purpose."

After dinner, no one lingered.

The dishes were rinsed, not washed. The leftovers scraped into foil and forgotten in the fridge. Sam offered to take out the trash and never came back inside.

Helen stood by the window, arms crossed, looking out into the dark.

"It's just a house now," she said.

"No," Leah said quietly. "It's still her. Just scattered."

Misha turned off the lights in the dining room, one by one, until only the hallway glowed.

That night, Leah stayed behind.

She walked room to room, slowly, her hand brushing each wall like she was trying to absorb what hadn't yet left.

In the kitchen, she opened drawers looking for nothing in particular—and found something instead.

Beneath the oven mitts. Wrapped in oilcloth. Yellowed at the corners.

A letter.

Addressed in **Anya's handwriting**, unmistakable. Sharp but elegant.

To: R.K. Halem

Belgrade, 1938

Leah stared.

She opened it slowly, breath caught behind her ribs.

Inside: a few pages written in a language she barely knew—lines of slanted script, phrases repeated, underlined. One sentence at the end in English:

"I kept your name, even when he gave me his. He never asked. You never came. I told no one. But someone should know."

Leah read it twice. Then again.

R.K. Halem.

Not Kerem. Not Yusuf.

Someone else.

She folded the letter carefully and placed it into her coat pocket.

Outside, the fig tree groaned in the wind.

Inside, the house was dark. Still. Breathing.

And the truth, long dormant, had begun to stir again.

WINTER, 1973 – QUEENS, NEW YORK

Leah did not sleep the night she found the letter.

She lay on the living room couch with a blanket over her legs and the folded pages pressed flat beside her on the coffee table, as if proximity might reveal meaning. The house creaked and sighed above her —the same house where Anya had boiled herbs and whispered songs to seeds, where Yusuf had stood at the window watching years pass like ghosts through bare branches.

And now, here was this:

A name no one had spoken.

A letter never sent.

A truth never told.

R. K. Halem.

Who was that?

Not Kerem. She had seen that name before, heard it in the edges of Anya's stories, in the burned remains Yusuf had once left in a cedar box.

This was someone else.

Or... maybe the same someone, twice rewritten.

By morning, she had translated only fragments.

She had pulled out Anya's old Russian dictionary—the one with pages stained by time and tea—and tried to piece the sentences together phonetically, line by halting line.

What emerged was not clarity, but **emotion**:

Grief. Longing. Anger disguised as apology.

"I waited by the river for three nights."

"He loved me quietly, and I let him."

"If they ask, tell them I was faithful in name only."

These were not the words of a woman at peace. These were the words of a woman split in two—between men, between continents, between lives stitched and restitched to look seamless.

Leah did not tell anyone about the letter.

She carried it folded in the inside pocket of her coat, close to her chest, like a relic or a weapon. She took it with her on errands, on subways, to the library, to bed. She dreamed of train stations and doorways. Woke up once with a name on her lips—**"Rako."**

She wasn't sure if it was a real name or one her mind had invented to fill the gap.

At the Queens Public Library, she found maps.

Belgrade, 1938.

It was still Yugoslavia then. Still cracked by war, but not yet broken apart.

She searched immigration records, passenger lists, border changes. She asked the research librarian if "Halem" was a common name in Serbia. It wasn't. She asked if someone could enter America under one name and live under another. The librarian gave her a long look and said, "All the time."

Leah wrote in her notebook:

Yusuf Halem = assumed name?

Who was R.K.?

Did Anya marry twice? Or only once?

Did she choose Yusuf?

Did Yusuf know?

The questions piled faster than answers.

But what stayed with her most was the final line of the letter:

"Someone should know."

It didn't say *forgive*. It didn't say *remember*.

It said *know*.

One night, weeks later, Leah brought it up casually—too casually—at the dinner table with Helen.

"Did Grandma ever mention someone named R.K. Halem?"

Helen blinked.

"No. Why?"

"I found a letter in her things."

Helen tensed. "What kind of letter?"

"Unsent," Leah said. "Addressed to Belgrade. Dated before she and Grandpa were married."

Helen sat back in her chair. She picked up her wine glass, put it down again.

"She never mentioned it," she said finally. "But that doesn't surprise me."

"Why not?"

"Because she was a woman. And women back then learned to lose things before anyone could call them secrets."

That night, Leah sat with the letter again, this time by candlelight— her own small nod to the Thursday rituals she'd watched Anya keep with such quiet discipline.

The house felt colder than usual. The fig tree outside was black against the night.

She reread the letter once more, carefully now, as if it might vanish.

At the bottom corner of the last page, in faded pencil, Anya had scrawled a line in English, as if meant for someone in the future:

If anyone finds this, ask what came before Yusuf.

Leah closed the letter.

She looked around the house.

The walls that had held generations.

The rooms that had seen birth and betrayal and soup and Sunday and silence.

The house did not answer her questions. But it gave her permission to ask.

She reached for her notebook and wrote only one sentence:

I will find out who she was before she became ours.

And with that, the story that had begun on a ship across the Atlantic, through tenements, war, silence, and survival, shifted again—

toward a new chapter.

Toward a forgotten name.

Toward a truth that refused to stay buried.

WINTER, 1973 – QUEENS, NEW YORK

The snow began as a whisper—flecks of white drifting past the windows like feathers from a distant pillow fight. No one noticed at first. The forecast had promised "light flurries." But by late afternoon, the sky had dropped so low it seemed to be pressing its entire weight down onto the earth.

By dusk, the streets were buried. Cars hunched beneath thick mantles. Power lines sagged. The mailbox at the end of the block disappeared entirely. It was as if the world had been erased, one slow inch at a time.

Leah stood at the window and watched it fall—mesmerized by how quiet the end of a day could feel when all the clocks had given up.

"We're not going anywhere tonight," she said.

No one disagreed.

Inside, the house groaned with memory. The radiator hissed inconsistently. The windows sweated, then froze. In the kitchen, a leak tapped steadily into a metal mixing bowl like a forgotten metronome.

The rooms had thinned out over the past months—no Anya at

the stove, no weekly meals, no guests coming or going. Just boxes now. Stacks of photo albums wrapped in twine. Drawers left ajar. The space no longer felt lived in—only used, like a coat borrowed too often.

It was Leah, Helen, and Sam now. Three pieces of the same story that no longer aligned.

Helen wore one of Anya's old sweaters—wool, cable-knit, loose at the shoulders. She said she was cold, but Leah knew better. Sam sat on the floor by the fireplace, back against the wall, long legs stretched out, rolling a cigarette between his fingers without lighting it.

The electricity flickered once. Then again.

Then it went out entirely.

No one moved.

"Well," Helen said, half-laughing. "I suppose that's it."

They lit candles, found the old kerosene lamp in the hall closet. Someone boiled water from melted snow for tea. The house, stripped of light and distraction, settled into something deeper—something like breath.

"I can't remember the last time it was this quiet," Leah said.

Helen shrugged. "Quiet's not always peace."

"No," Sam said. "But it's honest."

They gathered in the living room. The fire was stubborn at first but eventually gave in, and soon the room filled with the scent of smoke and drying wool and lemon balm tea.

Leah sat on the rug, her legs folded beneath her. Helen curled into the corner of the sofa, cradling her mug. Sam paced for a while, then dropped onto the ottoman with a sigh.

"We used to do this," Leah said. "Before... everything."

"Before Grandma died," Sam clarified.

"Before she started fading," Helen corrected gently.

No one argued.

The silence came next—not forced, not awkward, but organic. It stretched like fabric, folding around them. There was no radio, no television, no ticking clocks. Just the house breathing, the snow outside pressing against the walls like a forgotten guest.

And then, as if drawn from the quiet, Sam asked, "Why didn't they tell us anything?"

Helen looked at him. "Who?"

"Your parents. Grandma. Grandpa. They lived through war. Crossed oceans. Changed names. Burned letters. And none of us know why."

"They didn't know how to tell it," she said. "Or maybe they thought we wouldn't listen."

Leah shook her head. "They told pieces. Just never at once. They gave us puzzles, not blueprints."

"I found a letter," she added after a long pause. "From Anya. Hidden in the kitchen drawer. Addressed to someone named R.K. Halem."

Helen blinked. "Not Yusuf?"

"No. Someone else. Dated before they married. Before they came here, I think."

"What did it say?"

"Not enough. But too much."

The candlelight softened the edges of their faces. They looked like portraits from different centuries—Helen with her high cheekbones and tired eyes; Sam, restless and sharp-jawed; Leah, a mirror of Anya in quieter times.

"She was someone before she became our version of her," Leah said. "And I don't think she ever stopped being that someone. She just made herself smaller so the rest of us could fit."

Helen stared into her tea. "I think I hated her for that. For disappearing into what we needed."

"You didn't hate her," Leah said. "You resented the silence. We all did."

The fire crackled.

Outside, the world vanished inch by inch.

Inside, the past came closer.

They began remembering out loud.

Helen told stories she hadn't told in years: the time Anya stayed up all night sewing her a dress for a school dance; how Yusuf used to hum to himself while shelling peas, unaware he was doing it.

Sam remembered how Yusuf let him use his tools before he could read. How Anya made him tea when he had his first heartbreak—no questions, just warmth in a cup.

Leah recited the recipe Anya had once whispered: *two parts flour, one part grief...*

They didn't speak like mourners. They spoke like builders—each word a brick.

At one point, Helen stood up and walked into the kitchen.

She returned with a bundle of cloth—old aprons, Anya's shawl, Yusuf's wool cap. She passed them wordlessly to Leah and Sam.

"They should be warm," she said. "And they should be remembered."

Leah pressed the shawl to her face. It still smelled like thyme and soap.

They fell asleep in the living room.

Sam curled on the ottoman, arms crossed. Helen reclined in the armchair with a blanket pulled to her chin. Leah lay near the fire, the shawl over her shoulders, the letter tucked beneath her pillow.

The snow continued falling.

And somewhere in the dark,

a memory stirred—

not loudly, not fully,

but like something returning

after years of being buried.

MORNING AFTER THE STORM, 1973 – QUEENS, NEW YORK

By morning, the snow had stopped.

The world outside the windows looked remade—quiet, colorless, waiting. White drifts pressed against the porch rails. The street was unplowed, the mailbox still missing. But the silence had changed. It was no longer heavy. It was expectant.

Inside the house, heat returned with a stutter and a groan. The radiators clicked awake. Pipes moaned as if stretching after a long sleep.

The fire had died sometime in the night, leaving behind a bed of pale ash and the faintest scent of smoke woven into everything.

Leah rose first.

She moved through the house barefoot, her fingers trailing the walls like someone saying goodbye room by room. The kitchen smelled of old onions and colder days. The bathroom mirror was fogged not from steam, but from age.

She boiled water for tea and didn't wake the others. The house, for the first time in decades, belonged to her alone—even if just for an hour.

The letter sat on the table, unfolded. Beside it, her notebook. A list now three pages long:

- Who was R.K.?
- Was Anya ever married before?
- What did Yusuf know, and what did he choose not to?
- When did the name Halem become fiction?
- Who are we if we've inherited a story that was never true?

The questions didn't scare her anymore.

They were breadcrumbs.

And the house, in its stillness, had taught her to follow them.

When Helen awoke, she moved slowly, her joints stiff from sleep in a chair too old for comfort. She stretched, looked at Leah, and said nothing. There was no need.

They had already said what needed saying the night before, beside fire and snow and the soft collapse of decades.

Sam shuffled in last, yawning, hair a mess, wearing Yusuf's old slippers.

"I dreamed we were on a boat," he said. "Not going anywhere. Just rocking."

Helen handed him a mug of lukewarm tea. "That's family."

They ate a quiet breakfast of dry toast and leftover jam.

There were no new arguments. No plans for another gathering. Just bags to be packed and a house to be locked behind them.

Helen folded the afghans with practiced hands. Sam swept the fireplace. Leah washed the mugs one by one and placed them on the drying rack like relics.

When they were finished, they stood in the entryway for a long moment, facing the door.

Helen turned to Leah. "You're not coming?"

"Not yet."

Helen nodded, though her eyes clouded.

Sam looked between them. "You sure?"

"I'm sure," Leah said. "There's something I need to do first."

She didn't say what.

She didn't have to.

The front door opened with a sigh.

Helen stepped out first, coat pulled tight. Sam followed, his boots crunching the thin crust of ice on the porch.

Leah stood in the doorway a moment longer, looking back.

The dining table was bare. The kitchen window still fogged from the steam of boiling water. The hallway was lit with soft morning gold, catching dust motes mid-air like stars waiting for stories.

She whispered a single word, one no one heard but the house:

"Thank you."

Then she stepped outside, the letter in her coat pocket, her boots leaving the first new tracks in the snow.

She would not return for years.

But in her mind, she carried the blueprints.

The soft syllables of stories once told by candlelight.

The scent of dill and black tea.

The sound of her grandmother's voice, half in dream, half in memory:

"We are still here. We are still hungry. But we are together."

Now, together had changed.

But the hunger remained.

SOMEWHERE IN EUROPE, LATE SUMMER, 1935 – BEFORE AMERICA

Before he was Yusuf Halem, he had another name.

It is gone now—lost like smoke through cracked stone alleys, like the scent of cardamom in the folds of a sleeve. But once, in the city where he was born, that name had weight. It was stitched into the hem of a birth certificate, scratched into schoolbooks, whispered between brothers in the fields when dusk fell and war drums echoed faintly from across the river.

He had a brother.

Not Kerem. Not a cousin borrowed by need.

An actual brother—**Rako.**

Born two years apart. They shared a bed until they were ten, a pair of shoes until they were twelve, and a single silver coin they buried beneath the orchard tree to "protect the family" the night their father was taken by conscription.

Rako was fire: fast-tongued, sharp-eyed, quick to laughter and even quicker to fury.

Yusuf—though he wasn't called that then—was quieter. A boy who loved books, who carved tiny letters into the bottoms of wood planks, who prayed with his head bowed even when no one else remembered the words.

They were meant to grow old together.

But war rewrites the endings of men.

The decision came in a single morning, delivered on the back of a bicycle, inside a letter that bore their village seal and no salutation.

Rako was named.

He had been seen distributing pamphlets near the university. Anti-government. Radical. Branded. The militia would come within the week.

"If you are smart," the neighbor warned, "he will not be here when they arrive."

But they had no papers. No visas. No passage. Just the orchard, their mother's ashes, and the silver coin still buried beneath the roots.

That night, the two of them sat on the flat roof of their childhood home and spoke like men already halfway to legend.

"You'll go," Rako said, his voice calm.

"We both will," said Yusuf.

"You know I can't. Not with a name like mine. Not with them looking."

"Then we change it."

Rako laughed. "And what? You pretend I am you?"

"No," Yusuf said. "I become someone else. And you become me."

They stared at one another for a long time. The silence between them was not fear. It was **grief rehearsed**.

They worked by candlelight for days.

Forged records. Copied documents. Rako had a contact in Marseille—a printer with loose ethics and tight fonts. They practiced answers to inspection questions. They split what little money they had: Yusuf would carry half sewn into the lining of his coat; the other half, Rako would use to vanish.

One name would leave. One would disappear.

One would live.

It was not noble.

It was **desperate.**

And it worked.

On the last night, they stood at the orchard, digging beside the tree until the coin surfaced—dull now, nicked with age.

Rako pressed it into Yusuf's palm.

"Take it," he said. "So you'll remember what we buried. And why."

"I'll send for you."

"No," Rako said. "You'll live for both of us."

When Yusuf arrived at Ellis Island, the ocean had already washed away his old name. He gave the one they had agreed on. A name that passed. A name that sounded quiet enough to survive.

He carried with him three things: a forged passport, a photograph of his brother tucked inside the lining of his coat, and the silver coin—cold and constant in his hand.

Years later, when Anya found the coin in the drawer beside their bed, he told her it was from "a cousin." When Leah saw the faded photograph once, he told her it was "just someone from home."

He never said the word **brother** again.

And when he burned the rest of the letters—those few Rako had managed to send before he vanished for good—he kept only one line, written in a hand identical to his own:

"Your silence will keep you safe. But it will not keep you whole."

He tucked it into a book he never finished reading.

That silence was what Leah inherited.

Not land. Not money.

But the space where truth should have been.

It passed down like a shadow sewn into the seams of every family story—an echo that made Anya's lullabies ache at the edges, that made Helen's voice go sharp when pressed too close to memory, that made Leah look at the mirror and wonder what it meant to carry the face of someone half-known.

And now the letter had surfaced.

The coin still lived at the bottom of a tin inside Yusuf's locked box, under scrap metal and a pair of rusted cufflinks. Leah would not find it for another year.

But the line had already been crossed.

She would carry the burden now.

Because silence, once cracked open, demands to be heard.

LATE WINTER, 1974 – THE HOUSE ON ELM STREET

The house was cold again.

Not the kind of cold that came with broken radiators or drafty windows, but a deeper, quieter chill—the kind that follows death, that lingers long after the body is buried, curling into corners like breath from a ghost's lungs.

Anya had been gone for just over a year.

But it felt longer. Or maybe it hadn't passed at all. Maybe time simply paused in the places she once filled—in the kitchen, where her breadboard still leaned against the wall; in the hallway, where her slippers waited faithfully by the door. Leah had tried moving them once. The silence that followed made her put them back.

The house hadn't been sold yet. There were too many signatures missing, too much grief too raw to navigate the paperwork. So it stood untouched, as if still waiting for its matriarch to come home from the market. As if no one had told the floorboards she wouldn't return.

Leah arrived alone that morning.

Snow clung to the edges of the roof, but the porch was clear—as though the wind had circled around it, choosing mercy for once. She unlocked the door, stepped inside, and inhaled the smell of a house that had not been lived in, but also not quite left: cold dust, tea leaves, old paper.

The letter was still folded in her coat pocket.

She hadn't shown it to anyone else. Not Helen. Not Sam. Not even Misha, who had left behind only a postcard with a Colorado address and a scribbled "be well."

It wasn't secrecy. It was **instinct**.

Some truths had to settle before they could be shared.

She made her way to the kitchen.

The table was still there, its surface worn thin in the places where hands had lingered—serving, folding, comforting. The candle stub Anya had last lit had melted into a silver puddle on its porcelain dish. Leah touched it gently. It crumbled beneath her fingers.

She boiled water. Not for tea—there was none—but for the ritual. Steam rose from the pot like memory, clouding the cracked glass of the kitchen window.

Then, she sat.

Unfolded the letter.

Read it again.

Each word a breath held for too long.

"R.K. Halem," it began.

But now she knew better.

It was a letter written not to a man, but to a memory.

The ink had bled slightly from time, the paper curled at the corners. But the writing was unmistakably Anya's—careful, slanted, a script trained in old church schools and perfected on laundry lists and recipe margins.

In it, Anya did not beg. She confessed.

"If this reaches you, then I have broken a vow I swore to keep when I took your brother's hand and crossed the ocean.

He said you were gone. That he had no choice.

I believed him.

And I loved him.
But I never forgot your name."
It was not long. Just enough to leave scars.
And at the end:
"If there is any justice in this life, you have lived.
If there is any justice in me, I will not burn this.
I will leave it where it can be found."

Leah read it three times. The third time, she did not cry.
Instead, she stood.
And walked to the bedroom.

The box sat at the back of Yusuf's old closet, beneath layers of wool and lavender sachets that had long since lost their scent.
It was heavier than she remembered.
She carried it into the living room and sat cross-legged on the rug.
The lock clicked open like a breath returning.
Inside: cufflinks, a prayer book, a dried flower pressed between foreign pages. And at the bottom, beneath everything else—**a coin.**
Silver. Worn smooth at the edges. Unmarked except for a single, shallow nick.
She lifted it, held it to the light, and felt her stomach twist.
This was not just an heirloom.
This was **proof.**

Her heart beat faster.
She turned back to the box.
Beneath the velvet lining was a false bottom.
She hadn't noticed it before.
With careful fingers, she pried it loose.
Inside: more pages. Thin, aged, and bound in string.
Letters.
Dozens.
Written in a hand she did not recognize—but one that mirrored her grandfather's, as if it had grown from the same root.

She didn't open them. Not yet.

But on the topmost envelope, in faded ink, was the first name she had ever seen written in Yusuf's old tongue:

"Rako."

Her blood turned to iron.

She stayed in the house that night.

Built a fire in the hearth with old newspapers and torn-apart cardboard. Slept in the living room with a blanket and the box beside her.

At some point in the dark, she dreamed of voices she didn't know.

A man whispering in a dialect she couldn't name.

A song hummed over fields.

Two boys sitting beneath a tree, burying a silver coin.

And then—footsteps.

Not in the dream.

In the house.

She woke.

The room was dark, except for the low, orange flicker of the fire.

She rose slowly, her pulse in her ears.

Then she saw it.

The front door—

not fully closed.

She crossed the room and pushed it shut. Locked it.

When she turned back, something caught her eye outside the front window.

Across the snowy yard, near the edge of the hedge where the snow was deepest—

footprints.

Fresh. Unbroken. Leading to the house.

But none leading away.

She stared at them, breath caught in her throat.

Behind her, the fire let out a soft, sudden **crack.**

She turned.

The top envelope—Rako's name—had **fallen from the box.**

As if someone had touched it.

She picked it up. Her hands were shaking.

And for the first time, she said it aloud:

"**I promise,**" she whispered, to the fire, to the box, to the silence that had shaped them all.

"**I will find the rest. I will find you.**"

Then she looked at the footprints again.

The wind began to rise.

And from outside the window,

a shadow moved.

The Last Thanksgiving had not yet come.

But it was close.

Thank you for reading *First Harvest*.

If this story moved you, reminded you of your own roots, or simply stayed with you after the last page, I'd be incredibly grateful if you shared your thoughts in a review. Your voice helps other readers discover the story—and keeps it alive, one memory at a time.

✎ Please consider leaving a review on Amazon, Goodreads, or wherever you found this book. Every word makes a difference.

With gratitude,

— Mira Halden

www.ingramcontent.com/pod-product-compliance
Lightning Source LLC
Chambersburg PA
CBHW072157060526
44654CB00046B/1329